ODD MAN OUT

A Western Novella

First independently published in the UK in 2021

This paperback edition published in 2025

Cover art & Illustrations by Anna Olofsson

Cover & book designed by Uncle Nafee

Uncle Nafee © All rights reserved. Including all illustrations and audios.

A CIP catalogue record for this book is available from the British Library.

ISBN: 9798493492020

This book is a work of fiction. Names, characters, places, plots, and incidents either are the product of the author's imagination or are used fictitiously, and any resemblance to locales, events, business establishments, or actual persons-living or dead-is entirely coincidental.

Please feel free to review this book without spoiling anything and without violating the original contents of this book as no part of this book may be reproduced, scanned, or distributed in any printed or electronic form without permission. Please do not participate or encourage piracy of copyrighted materials in violation of the author's rights.

When I was a teenager and writing stories like this one, I vividly recall spending the majority of my time behind the scenes figuring out how much money I would make if I was successful in selling my books. And my royalties will be deposited straight into my bank account each time I sell.
I used to pray to ALLAH and ALLAH listed to me.
Jeff Bezos showed up with Amazon! Now all I need to do is submit and publish my book, and each time it sells, money will be deposited into my account. However, I forgot to ask ALLAH to provide me the same wealth as Jeff—perhaps through writing!

This book is dedicated to Mr. Jeff Bezos

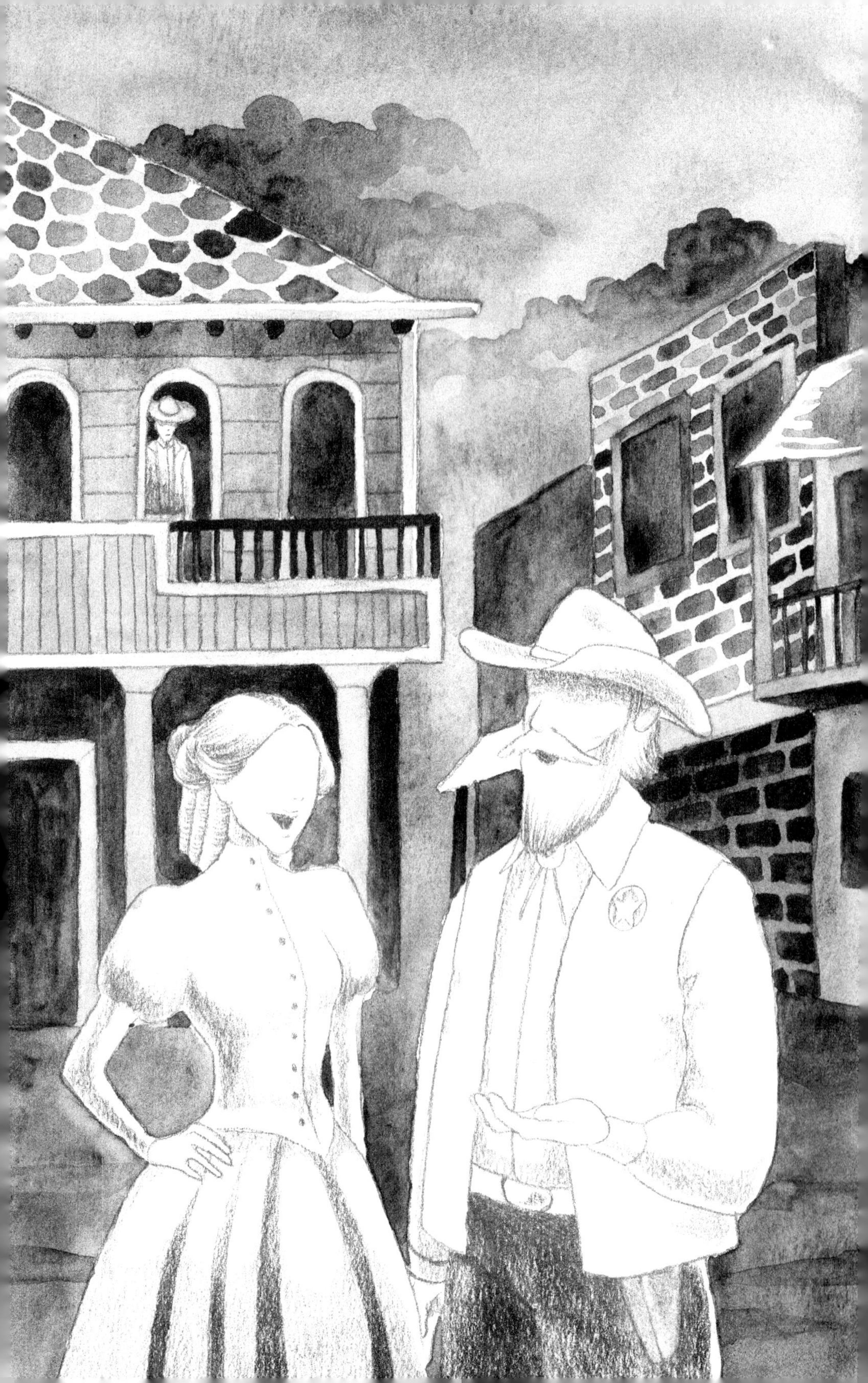

Illustrations by **Anna Oloffson**

This western novella revolves around an imaginary place called *Greentown* in the Wild West and the sudden and unexpected incidents that happened there. It was written long ago by a great fan of western fiction. It's Me, *Nafee*! When reading Western paperbacks, I thought I would try writing one myself. I was only sixteen that time. I dreamed that one day it would publish and eventually this one appeared as a novella in a special edition of a weekly national magazine, after some rejections from other publications.

Happy reading!

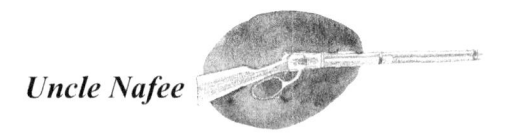

Uncle Nafee

CHAPTER 1

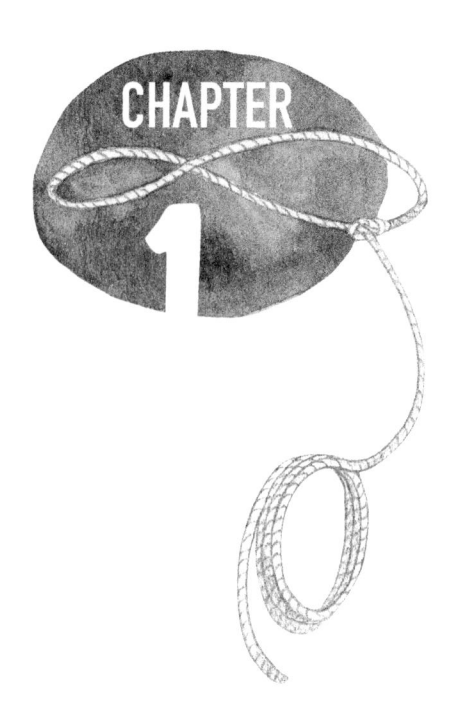

Martin was walking down the street when he suddenly heard a female voice calling out behind him. Abruptly, Martin turned around to see who it was.

She was rushing towards him.

As she got closer, Martin recognised her. She was the waitress at the restaurant where he just ate lunch. Her black velvet dress was shimmering in the sunshine.

"I'm sorry, miss..." Martin touched the brim of his hat and nodded at her. "Did I forget to pay for lunch or something?"

"No, of course you paid for it! But I didn't call you for that," the girl replied in a soft, gentle voice. She looked as gentle and sweet as her voice. Anyone who saw her would certainly take a second look at her pretty face.

"I think you forgot this." She handed Martin a piece of paper.

Martin took it, realising what it was, and glanced over it quickly... For a moment, he thought it might cause trouble, but when he saw her smile he realised he was mistaken.

"Don't worry," the girl reassured him. "I don't like to interfere in other people's business. That's why I came to return it to you." She looked at Martin with a wide, candid smile.

Although Martin was relieved, he did not say so. The truth was that he had left the piece of paper on the table on purpose, in the aim of getting the girl's attention. It was really only for a bit of fun.

He had half-expected her to be annoyed and when he had seen her coming to return the paper, he thought she might be coming to make a fuss. On the contrary, she appeared to want to get to know him and, although he was pleased, he couldn't help but wonder why.

"Thank you, miss!" Martin smiled back at her, "but may I know why you thought this trifling bit of paper so important?"

"I'm sorry Mr..."

"Martin, Martin Laslore."

"Yes, Mr. Martin. I don't think I've ever seen you in Greentown. I thought perhaps this was your first visit and that you didn't know the place. If that is the case, then I expect you'll be careful from now on."

Martin now understood.

She had come to threaten him, albeit in a very tactful way.

Did she always act this cool when she was angry? Martin wondered. He had thought that the girl was being friendly towards him, but in fact it was completely the opposite.

Martin pulled himself together, "Of course, miss, I will definitely heed your warning," he said quickly.

"I'm glad to hear that." Then the girl turned away and walked back to the bar, swaying her head in annoyance.

Strange! Martin thought to himself as he waved her goodbye, *Well, we will meet again for sure!* Muttering these words he tore up the piece of paper and threw it to the winds. He had not written anything special on it, just a single line: *You can only be compared to yourself.*

Well, he supposed he had a bit of fun!

But the girl was obviously smart; she could make trouble if she wanted. Maybe she hadn't wanted to waste the opportunity to show off her personality and that was why she had not said much. The slightest move on her part would be enough; the entire town could show him the fun he was thinking about!

Damn! Martin slapped himself hard on the head. Such extravagance thoughts always puts him in danger.

Anyway, Martin watched the girl going into the bar, realising that he didn't even know her name. Then he continued on his way, rolling a cigarette and putting it between his lips.

The footpath was dusty and dirty. Now and then unpleasant smells assailed his nose and the dust blew continuously into his face.

He pressed his bandana against his nose.

He observed both sides of the road as he walked along. There were many buildings on either side, some big and some small - stables, a general store, a saloon, a café, a law office, a church... everything was there.

But at that precise moment, Martin was thinking about a clean room in a hotel.

He had been travelling for at least thirty-six hours before he had at last discovered Greentown. First of all he had handed over his cherished black stallion to the stable hostler, and then he knew he too needed to rest. He thought he would take a shower and then have a good, sound sleep for three-four hours or so. That would be great!

Blowing out a cloud of smoke, Martin looked around him

to find the signboard of a good hotel.

He stopped at a crossroads and decided to turn right. A little further on, he caught sight of a huge building.

The wooden walls were discoloured and not in very good condition, but above the batwing doors there hung a glittering signboard, highlighting the "Saliman Hotel & Saloon".

The place looked welcoming enough. Martin threw down his cigarette and crushed it under his boot.

There were a lot of people walking along the road, all occupied with their own affairs.

Nobody was interested in a stranger.

They didn't even notice him.

Martin realised it was not unusual for these people to have an unknown person in their midst.

He walked slowly towards the hotel. The hotel had a perfectly-shaped balcony and stairs leading up to the door.

All of a sudden a man burst through the door and almost collided with Martin. He looked slightly embarrassed as his hat fell off his head.

Martin moved aside to let him pass.

The man tried to pull himself together but was unable to do so, obviously because he had been drinking far too much.

Martin picked up the hat from the ground and handed it

back to the man. He could see from the latter's ravaged face that he was seriously drunk.

"Hey man, pull yourself together!" Martin advised him, though feeling slightly repulsed.

"Damn!" the drunkard replied in an unsteady voice. "You can go now my friend!" Then he swung around as if nothing had happened and went on his way.

Martin went into the hotel.

There was a long counter with a shelf on the wall behind it where the keys were kept.

The bartender came forward to greet his new customer. He was a thin, black-skinned man with a pockmarked face.

"Howdy Mister! Welcome to the only best hotel in Greentown," the bartender welcomed him in a friendly voice.

"Thank you. I need a room," Martin said as he contemplated the saloon.

About ten people were sitting around, playing cards or drinking whisky and talking loudly to each other. Nobody looked at him.

"I have just one spare room at the moment, sir," the bartender told him, observing Martin's impressive physique.

"Has it got a shower?"

"Certainly, sir!"

The bartender selected a key from the numerous bunches on the shelf behind him and handed it to him. He indicated the stairs with a smile. "Your room's on the second floor. Number 14, sir."

Martin took the key and paid the bartender, informing him that he would be resting until the evening. Then he started going upstairs. The bartender was surprised to see him that he had no baggage.

"Mr. Martin?" he called out as he checked his register. So, the man knew his name now. "Looks like you came here empty-handed?"

"That's right, Saliman," Martin confirmed, looking over his shoulder with a smile. Although he hadn't introduced himself, he now realised that the bartender was also the proprietor.

"I'll talk to you again this evening Saliman."

Saliman smiled at the six-guns which were dangling from Martin's waist.

He knew that they were not going to last long!

CHAPTER 2

When the light started to fade from the sky, Martin went down. He had found it hard to get to sleep that afternoon, but fortunately there had been some books on the nightstand which he had skimmed through to pass the time before finally falling asleep. After his nap, he felt much fresher, both in body and mind.

Saliman's bar was now very crowded and Martin took a close look at everyone there. He saw that Saliman was busy at the counter taking orders and serving drinks.

Martin called a boy and asked him to fetch him a whisky.

There was an old newspaper on the table, which he glanced carefully.

Martin put the newspaper back on the table. He remembered that he had to go out and buy a few necessities. Moreover, he had made up his mind to have supper at that pretty young woman's restaurant. He felt confident that he would get around her quite easily.

Martin found it hard to forget the way she had looked at him and her sweet, unfaltering smile.

He had never thought about a girl so seriously before.

But Martin knew that he could not get mixed up with any girl, unless he managed to lead a more stable life. Then maybe he could think about it. But for now, Martin had to stay away from her and to stop even thinking about her.

Martin swallowed the rest of the whisky in one go and stood up.

He wanted to find out more about the town from Saliman, but seeing the huge crowd in the bar he decided not to bother him just then and paid his bill to the boy. He informed the boy that he would not be there for supper then stepped out of the hotel.

Greentown might as well have been called Cattletown. Martin had followed the North trail to get there and had seen several ranches along the way, surrounded by grassland. The larger ranches must have had at least seven or eight hundred head of cattle and even the smaller ones must have had more than three hundred.

First of all, Martin went to the stables to check up on his stallion. He was satisfied with the service and gave the hostler boy a tip as he left. In return, the boy revealed some fresh news from town. It seemed that many unwanted strangers had recently turned up in Greentown and there had been a lot of fighting and shooting. There was no more law and order in the town. Just a couple of days ago there had been a bank robbery and, before that, eighty heads of cattle had been stolen from Garry's ranch.

The news pleased Martin for some reason!

Martin left the stables, found a tailor's shop and ordered some clothes and a pair of boots, saying he would call by and collect them on his way back to the hotel.

The tailor was the spitting image of a chimpanzee and appeared to be a depot of fat! He asked Martin if he had come to town on business or if he were perhaps looking for work. Martin didn't reply to these inquisitive questions and simply put his money on the table. But as he left the store, he heard the man advising him to be cautious, "You should be more careful, stranger. There are certain people in this town who don't care about having a good reason or excuse to cause trouble."

Martin walked away respecting the tailor's words. It was hard for him to hide his smile as he didn't expect such serious words from this strange looking guy!

He also wanted to go to the general store, but he was tired of walking, so he went straight to the restaurant. He didn't know why, but he felt as if the pretty girl was calling him!

Martin hurried along.

The restaurant's name was **Jay and Jenny's Restaurant**, so he guessed her name was Jenny. Martin expected to see her when he went inside, but instead he saw a boy of about sixteen or seventeen, who was taking care of the bar. He looked very much like Jenny.

"Evening stranger! Welcome to *Jan's dug-out!*" Hearing his voice, Martin was sure that he must be Jenny's brother. But he could not see Jenny anywhere in the restaurant.

"Thanks Jan, I came to have some supper." Martin smiled. He put three dollars on the table and asked for the menu. "I want to eat until my stomach bursts!"

"Of course Mr...."

"It's Martin, Martin Laslore."

"Yes, Mr. Martin. You don't seem to be a hawker like a lot of the other strangers," Jan said in an indifferent voice. "Can I ask you something?"

"Well, yes of course." Martin was trying to find an excuse

to ask him about Jenny's whereabouts, so that he would feel a little calmer.

"Are you staying in town for long?"

"That depends. My pistols will help me to decide." Martin gave a smile by pressing his lips.

"But I assume you have some money and I guess you haven't come here to look for work."

Martin thought Jan was a bright young fellow.

"You're right." Said Martin but quickly switched to his own interest for a sec just before he asked about Jenny, "If I need some money, then I must go to the bank. Though I heard about the robbery and bankruptcy... "

"In that case, you can go to another bank instead."

Martin realised that if he wanted to find out about Jenny from the boy - tactfully or not – he would be caught out. Jan seemed to consider him to be quite the gentleman.

Forget about that girl, you fool! Martin's own conscience remonstrated with him.

He sat at the table and ate his supper hungrily. Then he gave a satisfied burp.

A hot cup of tea came almost immediately.

As he sipped, he looked round him, sizing everyone up, but still he couldn't get Jenny out of his mind. He wondered where she could have gone. Did her family have a ranch? If they did, maybe she had finished work and gone home.

Suddenly Martin was startled by a thud as the door opened.

Four boys burst into the restaurant.

They were wearing flannel shirts and Ski trousers. Their hats were hanging from drawstrings on their backs.

They looked like trouble.

Martin was drinking his tea and trying to ignore them, but all of a sudden he heard a noise like a loud slap.

He looked at Jan.

Jan was trembling, either from fear or anger, and his hand had gone to his cheek. Two of the boys had gone behind the counter. One of them had grabbed Jan's collar and was shaking him vigorously. He seemed to be the leader of the gang and was the one who had slapped Jan.

"Jan, you dared fight with one of my men," the boy said angrily. "So you must pay for it now!"

"Your people stole some cattle from us!" Jan retorted as he managed to pull his collar from his grasp. Martin could clearly see the mark on his cheek where he had been slapped. "Not only that, Larry and Cat behaved wrong with my sister."

"I also want to say something to Jenny too! And if she agrees..."

"You've said enough, Vic!" Jan was bursting with rage now. He pointed a threatening finger at Vic. "Don't you dare say another dirty word about my sister."

"Or else you'll have to call me your brother-in-law, I suppose!" The guy called Vic laughed jeeringly and the rest of the gang followed suit.

Jan was on the verge of punching Vic in the face out of sheer rage, but the other boys caught hold of him to restrain him.

Jan struggled in vain to get free.

Then Vic slapped him on his other cheek.

Jan screamed in pain.

The other boys started to laugh sadistically at seeing him so helpless. Suddenly it was as if a thunderbolt had hit the restaurant!

First there was the sound of a gunshot and immediately afterwards the noise of something breaking on the floor!

The floor was wet and there were pieces of broken coffee mug.

For a moment or two it was so silent inside the restaurant that everyone could have heard a pin drop.

"What's wrong Mister?" Vic shouted at Martin.

Everybody was looking at Martin now, as if they hadn't noticed him until now.

Martin pushed his chair against the wall and put his legs on the table, sorting a more relaxed seating position.

He was smiling at them, as if in mockery, and twirling his

pistol in his hand. There was smoke curling out of the barrel and disappearing into the air.

"My tea cup couldn't abide your nonsense, so it aimed right at your head," Martin explained in a matter-of-fact voice. "If the bullet from my pistol hadn't broken it, then maybe it would have broken your head, Vic!"

Vic shuffled uneasily and Martin fired his pistol again. Everybody was astonished to see Vic's pistol fall from his gun belt.

"Friends, just stay where you are and don't try to move again. And you two, I'd be glad if you would release Jan at once," Martin said in an ice-cold voice. "Jan, take those nasty things out of their holsters and hand them over to me."

Jan obeyed orders and the boys were too frightened to protest. Someone who could drop a pistol from its holster at twenty paces simply had to be respected. Nobody dared speak to him except for Vic, who frowned at Martin, "Hey Mister! Why are you nosing into our business?" he asked with disgust.

"Because, I don't like extra trouble around me when I am in good mode," Martin replied. "But we're not finished here yet. Jan," he went on, looking at Jan, "you have the mark of ten fingers on your cheek; I want to see the same on Vic's!"

Jan was smiling now.

He understood that he need not be afraid as long as he had a person like Martin beside him, so he walked towards Vic confidently.

"You're overdoing it, stranger!" said Vic aggressively, looking angrily at Jan. But Jan completely ignored this remark and went up to him.

After a moment a loud slap echoed round the restaurant and Vic fell to the ground.

"Bravo Jan, bravo! But what about his other cheek?" Martin asked innocently, clapping with the hand that held his pistol and looking as if he were really enjoying the whole thing.

Jan tried to pull Vic up to his feet, but Vic pushed him away and stood up by himself. His lips were bleeding. He wiped the blood away. The other three boys were standing like dummies, not uttering a word.

"I can't help congratulating you on your courage, stranger," Vic said seriously. "But remember that I'll get my own back some other day."

Martin put his pistol back into its holster and rolled a cigarette, pretending not to hear him. Vic looked at Jan menacingly. "And you, Jan, be sure you'll be seeing me again. I'm leaving now, but I'll be back!"

One of Vic's followers shouted out, "give us back our guns!"

"I guess you haven't yet returned Jan's cattle. When you've done that, then you can get your toys back, kid!" said Martin, nonchalantly.

"Hey look…" Vic's voice rose again, but he was interrupted.

"Jan, tell these guys to get out of my sight. Otherwise, if my pistol comes out of its holster a second time, there'll be blood all over this place."

The boys were afraid to say another word and turned to leave. But they were looking at Martin as if to say, *"Alright, but we'll meet again!"* And it looks like Martin just catches these words!

"I hope to see you again, my friends!" Martin echoed their thoughts as he bade them goodbye.

He looked at Jan, who was gazing at him in admiration. Jan had discovered that this *"gentleman"* was not quite as he had imagined.

Suddenly they heard the sound of the door opening and Martin saw Jenny coming into the restaurant. She was almost running and looking very agitated, as if she had heard some terrible news.

"Are you alright Jan?" Jenny ran to Jan and threw her arms round her brother. "For God's sake…!" She was sobbing. Tears were running slowly down her silky cheeks.

CHAPTER 3

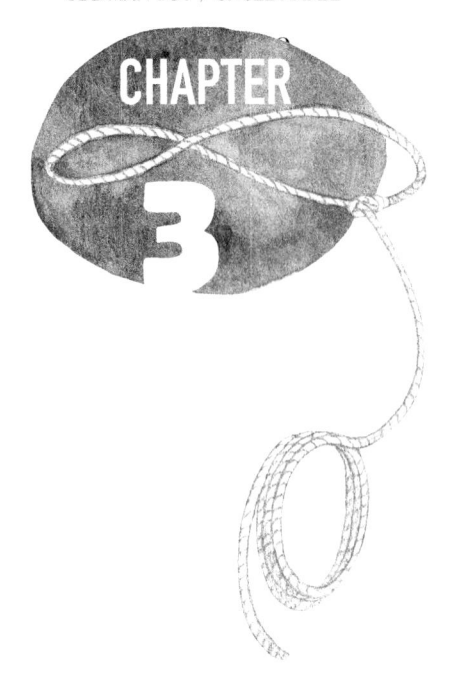

The sheriff was leaning against a pillar with his hands on his chest.

Although not really good-looking, he was a tall, well-built man whose demeanour gave off an air of self-assurance. His cool yet alert eyes clearly expressed that he was very cunning, the kind of man who, if necessary, would not hesitate to attack someone from behind.

The person he was waiting for came at last.

Jenny approached slowly, plunged in her thoughts. She

was thinking about the person who had saved her brother from Vic.

Martin was his name.

His handsome, yet friendly face kept coming into Jenny's mind.

Who was this man?

And why had he come to Greentown?

Unless it was for business or work, hardly anybody ever came to this town. Those who came were often rustlers or other kinds of outlaws. But was there anybody as charming and nice-looking as Martin? Certainly not!

"I beg your pardon, miss," the sheriff interrupted her contemplation. "I need to talk to you about something." He removed his hat and bowed to her.

"What's the matter, sheriff?" Jenny acted as though she was really surprised to see him.

That girl can't give up her habit of interfering! The sheriff swore silently to himself. Then he gave her a forced smile and came to the point.

"Miss Jenny, I heard there was some trouble at your restaurant yesterday."

"I guess you must have dreamt that up!" Jenny replied.

The sheriff ignored the remark. He was feeling rather embarrassed in her presence. He knew that if he wanted to talk to her directly then he could lose his job. So he pulled himself together and said, "Miss, you should beware of that new guy, Martin Laslore. You may not know, but…"

Jenny stopped him right there.

"I was just thinking about a way to replace you with him," she said, looking him straight in the eye.

"You can do that, miss, but…"

"Sheriff, I hope you know by now that I don't have any time to waste talking about such nonsense. You've told me what you had to tell me and I have listened. You may go now." Jenny said this lightly, though she realised that she was being a little insolent.

But the sheriff was not upset at all. Instead, he waited for Jenny to finish what she was saying.

"Please try to understand," he said solemnly. "I need to share some important information with you about this Martin guy."

Jenny did not reply straight away.

She saw that the sheriff was perfectly serious and she wondered what the matter was.

Why was he so concerned about Martin?

Was Martin actually a law-breaking vagabond?

Of course, it could also be possible that he was actually innocent but a convict in the eyes of law. You can never tell a person by his appearance or guess what is in his mind.

Jenny nodded at him and said, "Alright. Let's not waste

any more time - tell me what you want to say."

"Not here, miss. Let's go to my office."

Jenny hesitated for a moment, but finally agreed to go with him.

The sheriff smiled at her indulgently.

He indicated that Jenny should walk in front of him and followed her to his office, which was not far away.

Martin looked out the window of his hotel room and saw that his lovely Jenny was talking to a man. The man looked as though he was eager to impart something, but Jenny was not paying much attention.

Who was this man and what did he want from Jenny?

Why did the man seem familiar to him?

Ah, now he remembered - he was that drunk guy who had collided with him yesterday outside Saliman's hotel. But what did this drunkard want from Jenny? Though at present, nobody could really label him as a drunk; he was quite the gentleman.

It's disgusting! Whatever am I thinking about? Martin murmured to himself.

After all, Jenny was a respectable girl and the townspeople admire her. Anybody had the right to talk to her if they wanted to.

Martin watched Jenny accompanying the man to the

other side of the footpath and going into a lane on the right. She seemed to be asking the man something and they gradually disappeared from view.

Martin moved away from the window, repressing his thoughts.

There was a small mirror on one of the wooden walls in his room and he scrutinised his face closely.

For several days he had not been able to shave and he was beginning to get a rough beard, which made him look older than his age. He looked about thirty when, in reality, he had only just turned twenty five. The advantage was that his newly grown beard and moustache hid his face and made it difficult to recognise him. Martin preferred it that way since he didn't want people to show too much interest in him. Until now, anyone who had shown excessive curiosity had not been allowed to live.

Thinking about the past, a wicked smile spread across his face.

He looked over his shoulder and glanced at his money belt that was lying on the bed. It contained exactly five thousand dollars. For now he could put the money in a bank and start doing his job. As far as he could judge, the inhabitants of Greentown weren't interested in interfering in other people's business. If that were true, then he could think about getting a small ranch nearby. However, he knew that to do that, it would be impossible to avoid the influential people in the town and then there would probably be problems with lawsuits. Then again, it might not be so much of a problem if he could strike up a friendship with them. There had been certain problems in his past, however, which, if he could not clear them up, would prevent him from going ahead with his plans. It seemed that the right time had not yet come to deal with the mess. Maybe it would sort itself out when the right time came, or maybe someone else could sort it for him. The main thing was that if everything went according to plan, then Martin could manage the rest of it easily. He would not need anybody else...

There was a loud knock on his door, which jolted Martin back to reality. He heard Saliman's voice outside and opened the door. Saliman was standing in the corridor with a smile on his face. He was a very thin man and so tall that he would probably have to bend a little to enter the room. But Saliman did not go in. He stood at the door and said, "Good morning sir, I hope you slept well."

"Very well, thank you. Your hotel is really nice. I'm very satisfied." Martin said, leaning on the door frame.

"Thank you very much, sir." Saliman's smile spread even wider. "Sir, Mr. Robertson is here to see you. He's waiting for you downstairs."

"Robertson?"

"He's the foreman at the *Triple J* ranch. Perhaps Mr. Jerri sent him."

"Are you talking about the owner of *Jay and Jenny's Restaurant*?"

"Yes indeed, sir!"

"Alright, tell him to wait a minute. I'll come downstairs." Martin closed the door, leaving Saliman still standing there.

He went to the bed quite calmly and took off his shirt. His muscly, hairy chest, and wide shoulders displayed unusual strength.

He took the money belt from the bed and strapped it onto his shoulder. Then he put on one of the new flannel shirts that he had bought from the tailor's shop the day before and tidied himself up. At last he emerged from his room with his gun belt hanging from his waist.

He was wondering for what reason Mr. Jerri might have sent for him. He thought that the only plausible answer was that he wanted to thank him for saving his only son. Perhaps he wanted to warn him about Vic as well. Yes, it would be alright if that was the case - but if the man suddenly asked him about something else? As a rule, Martin could not bear excessive interest in him, but for something like this he supposed it would be alright. It was normal to show a little interest in a new face.

Martin went slowly downstairs. He saw a short, stout man with a plump face standing in front of the counter. He was wearing cowboy clothes, with a hat on his bald head. He must have been forty or fifty years old.

The man heard the sound of footsteps and turned towards the stairs. He smiled at Martin and welcomed him warmly.

"Hello Mister, you must be Martin?"

Martin smiled too and held out his hand.

"You recognised me right away, Mr. Robertson."

Robertson shook his hand and looked at him reproachfully.

"Nope!" he exclaimed, "You must call me Robert." Then he looked at Martin from head to toe, as if to make a thorough examination. He raised his eyebrows. "Hm! Jan didn't lie to me - you really are a handsome man!"

"Thank you," Martin replied, unembarrassed by the praise. He knew that people like Robert were usually very friendly and genuine. They were the kind of people he appreciated.

Also, they did not generally create trouble intentionally, although they didn't usually spare troublesome people either.

They left the hotel together. Robert's horse was hitched to a rail. Martin saw that his stallion was standing beside it, as he had requested to the hostler boy earlier. The men mounted their horses and moved off slowly.

They had not gone very far when they heard a loud cry and saw smoke rising up above the stores on the east side of the town.

They spurred their horses and galloped towards the smoke to find out what had happened.

As they got closer to the scene, they could hear people screaming in fright. It was clear that there had been an outbreak of fire and everybody was rushing about trying to extinguish it.

CHAPTER 4

A man entered the sheriff's office, completely out of breath.

He looked as if he were being chased by a ghost and had to run as fast as his legs could carry him to get there! He was panting heavily and could hardly speak. When he saw that Jenny was talking to the sheriff, he lost his nerve and seemed unsure about what should be done in such a situation. But the sheriff rescued him from this awkwardness.

"What is it?" the sheriff asked, realising that it was

something important. At any other time, he would have bawled the man out for surging into his office without permission.

The man pulled himself together and wiped the sweat off his forehead.

"Sheriff, Navice's newspaper stand has been burned to the ground! I heard that it was done intentionally!"

"What?!" The sheriff leaped out of his chair.

"Yes, poor Navice is in despair."

"What's that you say? Let's go there quickly!" The sheriff picked up his hat from the desk and addressed Jenny.

"Sorry miss, I have to go. But, think about what I said. I'll see you later."

With that, he hurried from the office. Jenny stood up to leave as well. The bringer of bad tidings nodded at her. Then he turned and rushed back out of the office.

When the sheriff arrived on the scene, the onlookers had calmed down. There were only a few people talking with lowered voices.

He looked at Navice's stand, without dismounting his horse. The stand had completely collapsed and nothing remained of it except a heap of black ashes. The smoke was still blowing in the wind.

Two of the adjacent stores had also been affected by the

flames, but had fortunately not suffered too much damage.

The sheriff looked at the crowd of people and got off his horse and walked towards them.

When they saw the sheriff coming, the disgruntled mumbling turned into inaudible whispering.

The sheriff spotted Robertson, the foreman of the *Triple J* ranch. Robertson was standing there looking annoyed, with Martin at his side.

"Sheriff!" Robertson called out rather resentfully, "please can you do something about these stupid people!"

"What's going on here?" the sheriff inquired.

"They're all claiming that I'm the one who set fire to Mr. Navice's store..." Martin answered, although he did not seem over-worried.

"...which is not possible," Robertson added, "since I brought Mr. Martin here just now from the hotel."

"No, that's a lie!" someone shouted from the crowd.

"It was him! He set fire to the store!" someone else chimed in.

Again there was a hullabaloo, but the sheriff put his hands up and protested with a roar, "are you going to stop that?!... Where is Navice?"

A man appeared from the midst of the crowd. He was short with bloodshot eyes from continuous crying.

"May I know what you have to say?" the sheriff asked

him.

"Yes, Sheriff, this man set fire to my store!" Navice pointed his finger at Martin, but the latter did not react. He was standing very still and erect.

"How do you know? Was he next to you when it happened?"

"No, he was running away after setting the stand on fire – I saw him then."

He took a hat from another person's hand and showed it to the sheriff. "When he was running away, this hat fell off his head."

The sheriff took the hat. Martin was surprised to see that it really was his hat and that he wasn't wearing a hat now.

Then he remembered that the night before he had heard some strange noises in his room. Now it occurred to him that a thief must have stolen the hat and that the thief must be very cunning...

Was it Vic?!

"Does this hat belong to you, Mr. Martin?" the sheriff asked him.

"Yes..." Martin hesitated a moment. "But I have no idea how it got here!"

"Because you came here with it!" Navice suggested angrily.

"Did you see my face?"

"Of course... I still remember your devilish smile."

"Don't talk silly, Navice! Think again, who did you see exactly?" the sheriff asked impatiently.

"I repeat that it was definitely this man."

"So..." the sheriff looked at Martin helplessly. "You must understand, stranger, that you have to come with me..."

"This can't be happening Sheriff!" Robertson protested. "You can talk to Saliman if you want."

"Everything will be done according to the proper procedure, Robert, but first things first..."

There was a loud cry among the people: "We need compensation!"

"Look, Sheriff, I agree to give compensation, if that will make things any better," Martin declared, "but I assure you I'm innocent."

The sheriff shrugged his shoulders.

"I'm helpless here. You must come with me. It's my official duty."

Martin didn't insist. He knew there was no point in saying anything more, though he was not really worried. He knew that only Vic would do something so stupid.

"Don't worry Mr. Martin, I am..." Robertson was trying to say something, but Martin stopped him with a smile. "Don't worry about me, there won't be any problem!" Then he looked at the crowd and caught sight of Vic's malevolent face and saw that his companions were with him as well.

There was a malicious smile on their faces! But Martin only winked at them and smiled.

Miss, Martin Laslore is a bounty hunter...

The words were echoing in Jenny's brain. This was what the sheriff had told her before she left his office.

A bounty hunter in Greentown!

That meant there was a possibility of huge chaos in the town. Bounty hunters did not wander around for no reason. Their job was to shoot notorious outlaws or fugitives and demand rewards in return. If Martin were a bounty hunter, then who was he looking for?

Jenny pondered for a while.

She didn't recall seeing any strangers in the town lately who looked suspicious or liable to be wanted. Moreover, all the people who carried out illegal actions had no fear of any legal steps being taken against them. Everybody did what they wanted to do in public. So there must be a reason behind Martin Laslore's arrival here.

Of course Jenny had not believed the sheriff at first. But when he put the wanted list in front of her eyes and said, *"I picked up this paper outside Saliman's hotel yesterday, disguised as a drunk..."* she looked and saw Martin's picture.

There was no reason to distrust the sheriff now.

No, it must be true. Martin Laslore must indeed be a bounty hunter.

If Jenny had been an ordinary girl, the sheriff would not even have bothered to warn her about Martin. Jenny knew this very well and she knew the reason behind it too. But she was not worried about that.

She had left the office almost immediately after the sheriff. She went to the restaurant and directly to the kitchen. When her father, Mr. Jerri, learned that Martin was a bounty hunter, he would have only one idea in his head and that would be to chase Martin away. He had been having trouble with the ranch lately and if there were more trouble on top of that, then it would become hard to stay in Greentown.

But why am I thinking about all this? Jenny scolded herself.

She washed her hands in the basin and dried them with the towel that was hanging in front of the mirror.

Suddenly she saw a person behind her in the mirror.

She sprang around at once.

"Johnson!" Jenny exclaimed happily. She looked appraisingly at the young man standing before her.

"You were supposed to stay in Glitter City today..." she started.

"Uh huh... I was supposed to be in the afterlife instead of Glitter City, and it's very lucky that I am standing in front of you now!" the young man joked.

"Don't say such things! Tell me what the matter is really," Jenny insisted.

"I've told you the truth, Jenny! I went to Glitter alright, but the Borhan's outlaws attacked us on the way. If that stranger hadn't turned up, maybe I would be..."

Jenny stopped him by pressing her finger to his lips. She went nearer to him.

"Don't talk like that! It makes me sick."

Johnson smiled at her and made as if to embrace her. But Jenny stood aside quickly.

"So tell me, what happened exactly?"

"We camped at Glossy Mountain and were resting by the fire. Suddenly, out of the blue, bullets started raining down on us and we were so startled that we didn't have the time to defend ourselves. There was a horseman near the trail and he came to help us. Honestly, if it hadn't been for him we wouldn't be alive right now. The belongings were unharmed, but Dowdy was slightly injured."

"It's a relief that nothing much was damaged," Jenny agreed. She sighed. "Did the man go with you?"

"No, I went on to Glitter. He asked me if there was any town nearer, so I told him about Greentown, so he must have arrived before us. Do you know who came to town recently?"

"A man called Martin," Jenny replied. There was sweat on her forehead from anxiety.

"Oh yes! That was the name the man gave us. Good, I'll find an opportunity to thank him!"

"But before that, tell me if you've had your breakfast or not," Jenny said, changing the subject. Johnson frowned and put his hand on his stomach.

"How can you imagine that I'd have breakfast anywhere other than at your place?!"

He caught hold of Jenny from behind and put his arms around her. Jenny tried to wriggle free. At last Johnson gave up and they both burst out laughing.

Jenny gave him a big hug, smiling and blushing.

Johnson was the son of Robertson, the foreman. She wasn't sure about his feelings, but she knew quite well that he was the only man she could ever love.

When she dreamed about the future, she knew he was the only man she could trust...

CHAPTER 5

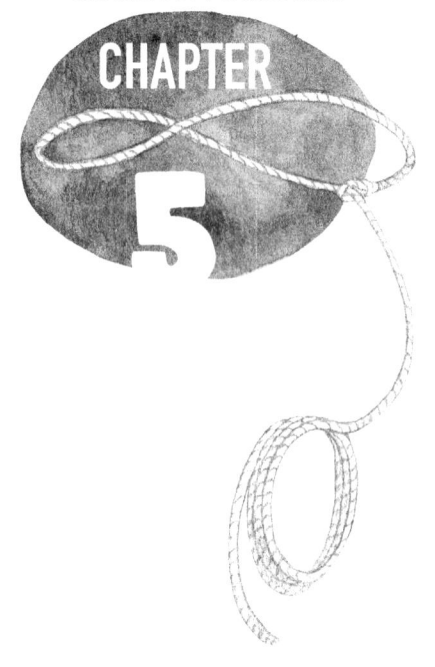

Martin did not have to stay long at the sheriff's office. With Robertson's help, he soon obtained his release. Even so, he still had to pay for his bail. As he left the office, Martin noticed that a stranger, leaning on a pillar, was looking straight at him. The man then quickly merged into the crowd. Martin and Robertson mounted their horses and headed towards the *Triple J* ranch.

They were cantering along the rough trails when Robertson asked Martin, "Mr. Martin, may I know where you were the day before yesterday? I mean where did you come from?"

Martin smiled at him.

"I was in a town called Glitter City," he replied, "where I stayed for a couple of days before coming here directly."

Robertson looked at him with a hint of curiosity on his face.

"Glitter City! Strange!! Now, I hope you won't deny that you also stopped at Glossy Mountain and that you saved a wagon along with a bunch of people from a group of ambushers?"

"And over chief Johnson is one of your people. I heard the name of this town from him. Otherwise, I would probably be roaming aimlessly towards South Capasi by now. That young man told me that he was going to Glitter City on behalf of *Triple J* ranch. By the way, has he returned?"

"Yes, he returned this morning. As a matter of fact, he's my son. He told me all about it."

"What more did you hear?" Martin asked him with acute interest. Suddenly he felt a little numb.

"I didn't ask him anything else," Robertson replied, "but, I imagine that Jerri has already made his investigations about you. When strangers arrive in the town, he's got into the habit of finding out as much as he can about them. He lost a lot of money in the bankruptcy a couple of days ago. We assume it was an inside job and that some of his employees may also have helped the rustlers steal the cattle. These incidents only take place when some new guys come to town and they disappear almost immediately. Because of this, Jerri has decided to keep an eye on all strangers. But..."

"But I hope you don't think that about me?" Martin interrupted him. "You can be sure that Mr. Jerri will introduce me to you in a completely different way."

He smiled at Robertson as if he were joking.

Martin felt relieved when he heard nothing that he might have expected.

He was more comfortable now.

The foreman did not ask him anything further and he shrugged his shoulders. After a while he resumed the conversation but on a different subject.

"I think that Vic wanted to send you to jail!"

"Why do you say that?"

"You've just arrived in town so you're not acquainted with the people here. I'm convinced that Old Nick bribed Navice in order to send you to jail."

"Hmm... and that's why I don't want to waste my time by charging Navice!" Martin nodded. "But remember, if you don't pay him back then he won't let you sleep in peace. He doesn't have the guts to pull the trigger, but he sure knows how to annoy someone."

"I don't have any problem with that, in fact I'd rather

enjoy it. As long as I'm here, I can play with that brat - I'll consider it as a kind of exercise."

"Well said!" Robertson approved, pulling the reins to slow down.

Martin looked around him. A little further along the trail, on the right, there was a small lake among the meadows. On either side of the lake there were ornamental gardens and, right beside it, a huge ranch enclosed by fences.

Beyond the ranch, the surroundings were magnificent, as if painted in water colours. Cattle were grazing in the pastures and on the north side of the ranch there was a big forest of cottonwood trees.

"We're here, this is our ranch," the foreman announced as got out of his saddle.

Martin hitched his horse and followed the foreman quietly. There were bushes and plants in the fields that Martin could not name, as well as a lot of eucalyptus trees scattered here and there.

Martin followed Robertson through the gate. A narrow, concrete path crossed the garden and led to the ranch's store.

A thin, unhealthy-looking cowboy took their horses. More than five cowboys were in the stables, busy at work. There was a small shack nearby where it was apparent that the cooking was done; appetising fumes were rising up into the air. In spite of the mess, the worker's environment seemed quite comfortable.

The cooking shack, bunkhouse and various sheds were situated on each side of the narrow path.

There was a farm on the bank of the lake. The water in the lake glimmered in the sunshine.

Martin and Roberson went to the balcony on the outer part of the ranch house.

Almost immediately a man emerged from inside. His figure and build were exactly like Robertson's, and apart from his clothes, which were elegant and refined, he could easily be mistaken for Robertson's twin brother. His skin was sunburnt and he had fair hair and a moustache.

It was clear from his imposing bearing that this was Jerri, the owner of the ranch.

He frowned when he saw Martin beside Robertson. His face looked a bit like Jenny's and his eyes were the same shape and colour as Jan's.

"A new guest in our town, Jerri!" Robertson gestured towards Martin. "But your face is telling me something else."

"You two sit down," Jerri indicated a bench, and sat in a chair himself. He examined Martin from head to toe.

"Why are you so late, Robert?" inquired Jerri.

"There was a bit of trouble in town," Robertson

explained as he hung his hat on a hook on the wall. "You know! But tell me what the matter is."

"I'll tell you... Howdy Mr. Martin. Nice to meet you in person."

The rancher smiled at Martin. Martin nodded back at him respectfully. He thought that the man had sent for him out of courtesy, but the conversation soon proved to the contrary.

Martin, who had remained standing, now sat down on the bench. He felt quite safe in this place.

"First let me express my utmost gratitude, Mr. Martin, for saving the restaurant and preventing Jan from fighting with Vic. You also saved Johnson from great danger..." Jerri pulled something out of his pocket.

"I am only doing my job, Mr. Jerri. I am..."

"Son, I think I understand what you're saying," Jerri interrupted him, "but the matter is slightly different. You've come from the West, so maybe you grew up in rough territory and that's why you take more time to understand the situation and how to work things out." As he said this, Jerri handed some papers to Robertson. Robertson looked at the papers attentively, his bald head shining as he bent forward.

"What are you trying to say, Mr. Jerri?"

Martin really did not understand what the rancher was

trying to get at, but now he was beginning to suspect something fishy.

"Think hard, Mr. Martin. Immediately after you got to town you had a bit of trouble. Then there were some other unexpected problems you had to avoid. But although you might not believe it, the town wasn't like this just a couple of months ago. The townspeople and the ranchers – we all lived here peacefully. Everything was in order. But now we keep experiencing crimes. Suddenly there are more cow thieves than ever. Bank looting has increased and new strangers are coming into town too often. I don't know who is behind all this, but it seems like some opportunists want to turn this town into their own territory. At least that's what it looks like."

Martin shifted rather uncomfortably on the bench. He guessed that his true identity was no longer a secret. For some reason, the rancher was trying to tell him that he was well aware of Martin's purpose for coming to town.

As Robertson lifted his head up from the papers, Martin looked at them both squarely in the eye.

"I hope you're not taking me for the kind of person who is responsible for corrupting your town?"

"Son, it doesn't suit you to act stupid! But maybe you didn't get the meaning of my words? So, I'd better tell you directly."

The rancher looked at Robertson, "What do you say Robert?"

"That would be best," Robertson agreed. "At least that's what I think after reading these."

Robertson indicated the papers that he was still holding. The rancher took them and gave them to Martin.

"Mr. Martin, take a look at these and you'll understand what I'm trying to say."

Martin had been right in his suspicions. Perhaps it was Johnson who had collected this information from Glitter City. If not, the leaflets must have arrived in town along with the newspapers. If that were the case, then there was no point in hiding his identity any longer.

"Mr. Jerri, now I understand. You think I'm a bounty hunter and that I must have come to Greentown in pursuit of some notorious criminal. If that were true, then there would indeed be a risk of disaster. You think that if there is any trouble because of me, then your town will be destroyed."

"That's right. If that happens, then things will be out of our hands, out of the ranchers' hands. So to save this town..." Mr. Jerri stopped as Martin stood up again.

"You are advising me to leave town, aren't you? But do you think..." Martin indicated the money belt suspended from his shoulders, "that I am still carrying out my past profession?"

"What do you mean?" The rancher looked puzzled.

"You should enquire more about me, I am worse than a vagabond right now. Yes, it's true that I was in that profession a couple of days ago, but all the money I've collected has made me dream of other things. So, I've given up being a bounty hunter. I hope that's clear to you?" Martin smiled at them.

"Bad boy!" Robertson exclaimed.

"Does this mean that you've decided to stay in town?"

"Of course! And I propose that you help me get a job. In return, I can assure you that there won't be any trouble in town because I shall be there to prevent it." Mr. Jerri and Robertson looked at each other. Then Martin bade the "twins" goodbye. He went to the stables to fetch his horse and thanked the cowboy. Just then he saw a woman at the window, who he guessed must be Jenny's mother.

CHAPTER 6

The second cow-hand, Johnson Hurt, the son of *Triple J* ranch's foreman Robertson Hurt, was not what one would call good-looking in a classical way, but there was something attractive about his appearance and physique which made people look at him twice. He was above average height, standing at about six feet tall, which caused the other young men in the town to show him a certain respect. They all knew that Johnson was more dangerous with his bare hands than when he was armed. Like his father, he was usually well-disposed towards others, but if he got angry, then beware!

Johnson never wore a holster unless it was absolutely necessary. He could cope easily with five men just with his bare hands, which was why the other young men usually kept their distance. However, Johnson was never unjust towards others.

In the case of Vic Rust, though, things were quite the opposite.

Vic was the son of Mathew Rust, the most influential rancher in the neighbourhood.

Johnson could not stand Vic and he knew very well that he was likely to lose control when Vic was near him.

Vic was aware of this too and for the sake of his own protection he usually avoided Johnson.

The basic rule of Greentown was that personal fights were to be carried out privately, which meant that Vic and his companions did not have the courage to go against Johnson. So Vic continued his crimes as sneakily as possible.

Johnson was rather surprised about Vic. It was presumed that the latter's two companions had been involved in the theft of eighty head of cattle from the *Triple J* ranch a few days before.

That very day, the boys in question were on the way to Glitter City with five or six of their branded cows when Jan caught them red-handed. It was of course possible that they had stolen just a few cows to get some money for gambling and were using the fact that there had been an outbreak of rustling to dissimulate their own theft. But if things went on like this, after a while employees would be stealing cattle from their own ranches to make themselves more money.

Johnson was worried.

He could see the huge difference between the Greentown of the past and Greentown now. As the days went by, the heretofore carefree life of the townspeople was changing radically. Just a couple of months ago there would have been no need to carry a gun, but now people are obliged to take firearms to ensure their safety.

Why did this happen?

What was the problem?

What was the source of this problem?

In the last two months, about two and half thousand head of cattle had been stolen from various ranches. The bank had been looted twice, causing some people to end up penniless. Nothing had been able to bring things under control and the thieves were continuing with their crimes.

The sheriff had done all he could to catch them, but to no avail. There was no sign of the bandits or even of their tracks. They succeeded in carrying out their robberies and then escaping without anyone seeing them.

It remained a mystery how the thieves could get away with stealing so many cattle!

The townsfolk couldn't understand it.

It was simply not possible that it was Borhan or some other gang. There must be some powerful outfit behind all this, who were hiding in Western Comanche or going through the counties with unbelievable skill. If this were the case, they would be able to disappear quite easily with the stolen cattle. But who were they? Who was responsible for this disaster? Who had hatched the plan to ruin this peaceful town after all these years?

Anyone influential in the town could be involved, which was an unsettling notion, but it was evident that someone from outside was pulling the strings. The person who had the ability and power to affect a nice quiet town within such a short time must be someone powerful.

Johnson didn't want to think about it; he could not imagine the fate of Greentown. He had left the restaurant, also perturbed by what he had heard there. Someone had informed him that a stranger called Martin had set fire to Navice's newspaper stand.

Martin!

It was a damned lie!

It must be Vic.

He heard that Vic had got into a fight with Martin at the

restaurant the day before, which meant that Vic must be wild to take his revenge!

He thought the sheriff would send him to jail. But Johnson knew that his father had taken Martin to the ranch and that there would be no problem for Martin if he stayed with him.

It was nevertheless a disaster that Navice's stand had been burnt down. All the newspapers from Glitter must be burnt to ashes!

That week, the townspeople would not be able to read the news. It was Johnson's responsibility to bring the bundles of newspapers from Glitter City every week, since there was no private newspaper in Greentown.

Navice could not be blamed either – if he had started the fire himself, he must have done it because he was frightened of Vic. However, if he got compensation from the municipality as well as some money from Vic's bribe, then he would not have wasted his time!

Vic must be the one who was responsible for all this. He had gone too far this time and needed to be punished. It might be a good idea to put him out of action for a couple of days. It was for this reason that Johnson was heading towards Parcy's bar to look for Vic. He knew that at this time of the day Vic usually spent his time at that establishment.

Johnson had listened attentively to Jan's account of how Martin had succeeded in taking away the firearms from Vic and his companions. The guns had been handed over to the sheriff, although they would soon be returned to their owners. But he need not worry, Vic would never have the courage to shoot him even if he wasn't wearing a gun belt, because there was no way out if he shot Johnson.

Johnson was walking quickly along the footpath. His horse was hitched to the rail outside the restaurant.

As he walked, an idea came into Johnson's head about Martin. As far as he knew, the latter was a bounty hunter. He had stayed at Glitter for two nights. But where had he been before that? Since he was travelling around from one town to another, apparently at random, might he not be pursuing a criminal? If that were true, this would explain his arrival in Greentown. And if the criminal in question were really staying in the town, there was a fair chance that Martin would find him. If he did, and it was this criminal that was creating all the trouble in the town, then a lot could be gathered from questioning him. This was Johnson's assumption, but it would have to be verified.

Johnson stopped in front of Parcy's bar.

There were no familiar faces around. He went into the restaurant without hesitation.

About ten people were sitting around the tables inside.

Most of them had just come in to get the latest gossip.

Johnson looked around him. He saw a complete stranger playing cards with Vic at the table in the corner.

Another man stood beside the stranger. He was short, but looked as if he were as strong as the other one. They wore identical black hats with sparkling chains dangling from them. Vic was also with one of his companions. Johnson could tell from Vic's annoyed face that he was not good enough at the card game they were playing and was evidently losing.

Johnson went up to the counter and the bartender came to serve him, looking rather surprised. Johnson smiled at the astonishment on his face.

"Don't be surprised, Parcy. I've just come to give one of your customers here a lesson!"

Parcy threw a glance at Vic's table.

He was an elderly man, but still quite upright for his age. His hair, eye-brows, and large moustache were all as white as snow and his face was creased in wrinkles. He was still able to do his job, old Parcy, but it was understandable that he didn't want any trouble in his bar.

"OK," Parcy said, "but I'd rather you spared me that here."

"I think you should call the sheriff," Johnson went on, noticing that Vic had suddenly risen from his seat.

"Cheat! You deceived me!" Vic roared at the stranger, banging loudly on the table.

"Perhaps I should take your advice...." Johnson heard Parcy saying, without taking his eyes off Vic's table. Everybody in the saloon was now staring at Vic because of his sudden change of behaviour. "Give me back all my money Mister!" Vic shouted at the stranger who remained seated.

"I'm sorry, buddy." The stranger now stood up too, looking Vic straight in the eye. "I've earned that money playing honestly."

Some of the customers started leaving the saloon, assuming there would be a fight. The rest of them stood around eagerly, waiting to see what would happen. The two strangers looked at everyone in the saloon.

"You have insulted us, Mister," one of them said. "We have no time for this kind of behaviour. We must go." Saying this, the two strangers turned to leave.

Vic blocked their path. A couple of his friends joined him.

"Look Mister," the first stranger said, no longer smiling, "you should know how to behave better with gentlemen."

"Gentlemen!" Vic exclaimed with a smirk on his face.

"What do you say, Vic, that we take off these 'gentlemen's' clothes?" one of Vic's companions suggested.

"He..." Another one was about to make an equally stupid remark when a pistol shot rang out.

For a moment there was a deathly silence in the saloon. Then all of a sudden one of Vic's companions crumpled and fell to the floor with a hole in his head!

One of the strangers had a six-gun. The smoke was still curling out of its barrel.

Vic's gang was rooted to the spot from shock. In fact, everybody in the saloon was completely stunned.

This was the first murder in the history of Greentown!

Everybody needed some time to digest the incident.

"Stay where you are, don't move!" the first stranger ordered, brandishing his pistol. "When we've gone, you can dance if you like. But first, let me have your guns - ALL OF YOU!"

Everyone obediently placed their guns on the table.

The stranger nodded to his companion, who methodically emptied the magazines of the pistols one by one. Then they both made towards the door, the man with the gun still treating the assembled company with his weapon.

Johnson was surprised to see that the two men could get away so easily after murdering someone. On the other hand, what could anyone do without a gun? Still, he was looking for an opportunity.

As the strangers passed in front of Johnson and moved cautiously towards the door, Johnson clenched his fists.

"If anyone tries to get to the door, they'll get a bullet through the head!"

"Friends, I will try to send some tablets right through the heads, whom I will see first from the gate!" The second stranger threatened with a shotgun. Johnson wondered how he had managed to hide it under his coat!

The two strangers had almost reached the door when someone suddenly jumped out from behind it and kicked one of them violently in the chest.

As they were completely unprepared for such an attack, the one who had been kicked fell over on top of the other one. The latter lunged towards Johnson as he lost his balance.

Johnson was ready.

He struck the man's hand that was holding the shotgun. The stranger screamed out in pain and had no alternative but to drop the gun. Johnson punched him in the face, causing him to sprawl across one of the tables.

Just at that moment Johnson heard another gunshot.

He recognised the sheriff at once.

The sheriff's bullet had gone right through the other man's palm, obliging him to let go of the six-gun. He tried to pick it up again, but the sheriff kicked him hard on the forehead. His body flew through the air for a second or two before crashing down on the bar counter with a huge thud.

The man who had been kicked by Johnson now saw his advantage.

He had picked up his gun and was pointing it at Johnson, ready to pull the trigger, when a bullet hit him in the throat. Before there was time to react, the other stranger was shot with a bullet which flattened him against the counter.

The sheriff was astonished!

He looked at his pistol, which was still in his hand. Then he saw that Johnson was staring at something, so he looked too.

Everybody watched with wonder that a person was looking at everyone with a rather curious face. It was evident that he was the one who shot twice; the two pistols in his hands still had bluish smoke twirling from them.

Who else could it be but Martin – Martin Laslore!

CHAPTER 7

About five hours later, four men were gathered in a small cabin. It was dark and rather creepy in the cabin. There was only one window, which was closed. In the corner, a rough-looking man was sitting on a chair. Two other men were standing beside him, leaning on the wall.

Their faces were cruel.

A man was walking up and down impatiently in front of them.

This was Sheriff Dalton.

He was looking anxiously at the man who sat on the chair. But the latter ignored his gaze – he was staring at the floor, thinking about something else.

The other two men were standing like statues, as if they were waiting for something to happen.

They were dangerous people.

"So you're saying that you're not involved in these incidents? Then who is, huh?" The sheriff broke the silence in the room. "All this time has gone by without anyone ever being killed, not even a fly, and then in a couple of hours not one but three people are murdered!"

"Try to understand, sheriff," the man on the chair said in a cool voice. "No matter who is behind all these incidents in the town, they definitely have reasons other than rustling or bank robbery. They want to bankrupt the influential people and force them to leave, so that they can take over the town. Do you get what I mean?"

"There's logic in what you say, Borhan, but I want to know who it is! You're the only person to have come from another place. And anyhow, who attacked Johnson that night in the hills?"

"I know the townspeople will suspect me first. But you at least know me well enough, Sheriff. I was an outlaw, I don't deny it, but I have come to your town to make my life better. The people aren't letting me do this. They think that they shouldn't take the risk of sheltering an outsider. But you have given me that opportunity, Sheriff. After that, how could you imagine that I would betray your trust?"

"I'm not suspecting you, Borhan. But as a dangerous outlaw in the past, you can perhaps guess the plans of other rough-necked guys. I want to know who is responsible for these acts!"

"Whoever it is, he must be very cunning. In my opinion, he's working in a group. But my people are keeping an eye on any strangers to the town. You can ask Dave – he has already marked some of them." Borhan indicated one of his companions beside him.

Dave had a hair-bun and a French-cut beard.

"Sheriff, one of the people I'm suspecting is Mathew Rust's foreman," he said. "I've seen some strangers around his place."

Reeve, Borhan's bodyguard, who was standing on the left, added, "but the person who is at the top of our special list… Well, we won't say anything about him right now, sheriff, because we need to keep tabs on him for a couple of days more."

"So you can relax," Borhan added, stretching his arms and standing up. "We'll help you in every way we can."

"Thank you. But did you recognise the two guys who were killed?"

"Those two have been meeting Carl, Mathew's foreman," Dave replied.

"What!" the sheriff shouted. "In that case we should make some investigations about Carl immediately!"

"You can try, sheriff. But one thing - no matter how good a person Mathew Rust appears to be, keep him on your list." Borhan smiled.

"You're quite right. I've already put his son, Vic, behind bars. He'll be there for a couple of days, I guess. He's a brat. It was because of him that one of his companions was killed.

"Oh yes, by the way, why did you spare that Martin guy?"

"Well, if it hadn't been for him, we would have been dead by now."

"That guy knows me well and I know him too. There's nothing wrong with him."

"He's a bounty hunter."

"Yes he was, but now for the sake of his livelihood …. I heard he's planning to stay here?"

"Yes, I think so," the sheriff answered. "At first I thought he was a troublemaker, but now I think differently."

Suddenly there was a brief knock and all eyes turned to the door. One of the sheriff's men came into the cabin.

The sheriff shook hands with Borhan and made to leave the room. As he reached the door, he turned round again.

"Will you be leaving tonight?" he asked.

"No, I'll be staying at Saliman's hotel," Borhan replied.

When the sheriff had left, he looked at his companions with a smile on his face.

"We don't have to inform him for now that we've already spotted the real criminal," he said. "You must all work to get sufficient evidence. Then..." Borhan added.

Outside, the sheriff was feeling more relaxed.

"Now, we have nothing to worry about," he announced to his deputy. "Borhan has taken all the responsibility; there will be peace in Greentown very soon."

But neither the sheriff nor Borhan had noticed the man standing on the pavement keeping a close watch on them.

That evening, the man going into the *Lifeway Bank and Insurance* was Mathew Rust's foreman, Carl Weapon.

The man looked like a living skeleton.

It was quite remarkable that this bony man could manage a whole ranch.

He must have been thirty or thirty five years old.

His two front teeth stuck out like a rabbit's and his body was as thin as a bamboo cane.

Despite his fragile appearance, however, Carl was a very cunning man. Even if his brain did not always work as it should do, he sometimes came up with some clever ideas.

Carl was not surprised to see strong security inside the bank. Armed guards were pacing up and down like soldiers. Carl went up to the counter whistling and gave the cashier a cheque. In return, he was given a wad of banknotes, which he counted carefully as he left the bank.

He looked sharply around him when he reached the road. Then he crossed over and went to an abandoned shed behind the tailor's shop. This was where "Mister" had told him to meet.

A lot of things had happened that day. Mister's work had been interrupted again and again. The day before Mister had ordered Carl to get rid of Rust's son, Vic. That was why Carl had sent Tom and Hins to the bar. The idea was that Tom and Hins would deliberately make trouble with Vic so that the fight would turn into shooting.

Carl had known Vic for a long time now. Although he carried a gun in his holster, his behaviour was worse than a drunk's. So either Tom or his brother Hins could blast off his head without difficulty. Managing the rest of it should have been as easy as pie. But nothing had gone according to plan. Vic was totally unharmed and instead both of the brothers were dead. Things could still be managed though, but if someone recognised the two dead men or found out that they were Mister's people, then it didn't bear thinking about Mister's reaction!

Carl shivered in fear for a moment. His heart was

pounding with dread.

He wondered what would happen when he went behind the tailor's shop.

Carl did not know what "Mister" was really called. Mister's own people called him "Mister", and so he did too. But it was obvious from the man's appearance and expression that he was cruel and unscrupulous. The cold eyes in his lupine face gave the impression that he had seen many deaths and was responsible for many of them too. It was evident that he would not hesitate to redden his hands in other men's blood, laughing happily.

Carl pulled himself together. He crossed the street and turned into the narrow road behind the tailor's shop.

He felt several pairs of eyes staring at him. He stopped in front of the shed. A man was leaning against a pillar in the shadows. Carl knew without any doubt that it was Mister. He looked at the man's face and relaxed slightly. A man of such power and influence wouldn't bother to make someone helpless for nothing, so there was nothing to be worried about. Mister would certainly not harm him without questioning him. Moreover, Mister would have never had any success without his advice. Thanks to Carl, Mister had set a wonderful trap to make it very easy to loot the whole town!

The plan had almost succeeded...

It wouldn't take long to loot everything.

Carl cleared his throat.

"Mister, according to your instructions I sent Tom and Hins to work. It was their own fault that they lost their lives. What can I do here?" He stopped.

There was no reply. So Carl continued. "We can forget about Vic for a few days and do something different," he suggested. "We could take Vic's father instead of Vic... that man is extremely honest, quite the opposite of his son! If we can get rid of him, then I will possess the whole ranch."

Carl waited for Mister to reply, but still no word passed his lips.

"The thing is, if we can control Mathew Rust, then we can take over almost half of the town. And it's a trifling matter to bankrupt *Triple J* ranch. We have a lot of things to sort, so if we can finish the Lifeway Bank by implementing it, everything will simply fall apart!"

At last Carl finished his speech, but there was still no reply.

Carl began to feel anxious again. He took a few steps forward.

"What's wrong Mister?"

Then he stopped right where he was and realised that something was amiss. He had been gesticulating with his hands as he talked, but now his hands reached for his gun.

Just then, the person in the shadows spoke in a thunderous voice, making Carl freeze with fear.

"Stay where you are, Carl. My people have got their guns pointing at you! It's Sheriff Dalton!"

The sheriff's huge body lumbered out of the darkness of the shed into the moonlight. Carl was more than taken aback to see him there.

"Don't be scared, Carl," said the sheriff. "Your plans are really marvellous. But right now, I want your gun belt."

Carl was totally lost for words. This time his brain failed to think up a solution. He panicked as he heard the sound of guns being cocked and began to unbuckle his gun belt.

Johnson got hold of Martin after the terrible incident in Parcy's Bar. He ignored all Martin's Excuses and took him to Jay & Jenny's restaurant for supper. He wanted to make the day a memorable one. In the end, Martin gave in to Johnson's insistence. He kept thinking about Jenny, but he had no inkling that his heart would be broken over supper.

Over the last twenty-four hours Martin had thought quite a lot about Jenny and imagined them being together, but all his dreams were shattered in an instant when Johnson, who was drinking a glass of whisky, suddenly said, "pray for me, buddy, when I become the foreman of the *Triple J* ranch and get married to Jenny..."

Afterwards, Martin could never remember how he had controlled himself. He had eaten his supper without showing any particular emotion and had managed to keep on smiling. Then he left the restaurant as quickly as possible.

On the way to his hotel room, he met a man in the corridor. He was so preoccupied with his thoughts of Jenny and Johnson that he didn't stop to wonder if he was familiar to him or not. It was only when he was closing his door that he realised that there were three people observing him closely.

CHAPTER 8

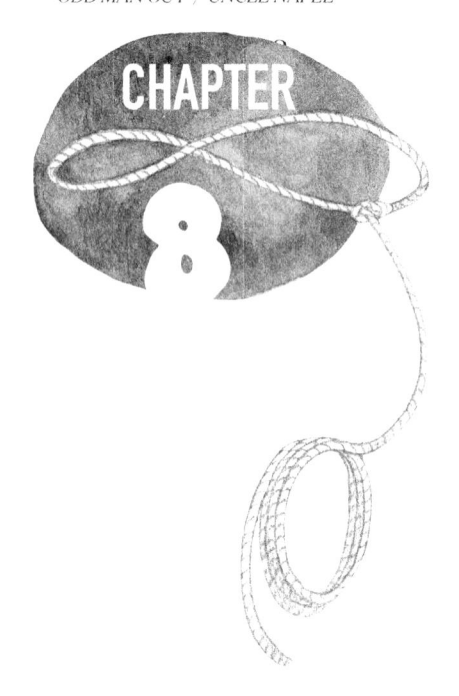

There was something preying on Borhan's mind and stopping him from going to sleep.

He was lying in bed, staring at the ceiling. He knew that Martin was in the next room.

He was worried about Martin. There was no sound coming from his room, but Borhan was sufficiently acquainted with him to know that Martin never slept continuously for several hours.

It seemed odd that he was sleeping unusually soundly.

Borhan wondered if there was something wrong. Had he

perhaps had too much to drink? That was very unlike him, and anyway he could hold his liquor. When Martin returned to his room, he had pretended not to recognise Borhan and his two companions in the corridor. Moreover, before Reeve and Dave left, they had knocked on his door and he hadn't answered.

Borhan felt there was something wrong. He knew that Martin had had supper with Johnson earlier that evening.

Wait a second...

What if one of his enemies had mixed some sleeping pills with his meal? And if that were the case, then the enemy in question would have only one reason for doing so.

They would want to kill Martin while he slept!

The reason was very clear now.

Borhan got out of bed quietly, so as not to arouse anybody.

He took his six-gun and a packet of poisonous Oxious dust powder from under the pillow.

Oxious powder was very effective for neutering an enemy. First it suffocated them and then, after a certain time, it would make them blind.

Borhan put the six-gun inside his trousers.

The room was lit slightly by the moonlight, which was filtering through the windows and making it possible to see everything in the room.

Borhan approached the door stealthily.

He could hear the sound of footsteps in the corridor. It sounded as if the person was walking on tiptoe and this made him suspicious. If it were someone from one of the other rooms or a boarder, then there was no need to tiptoe. Perhaps the person had a special reason for walking so quietly. Perhaps the reason that Borhan had thought about a while ago was true!

Death itself was coming to kill Martin!

Saliman's hotel was very quiet at night. Everything was abnormally silent. The glow of the lamps hanging here and there along the corridor created an atmosphere of fear.

The stranger was advancing slowly but surely towards room number 14. Everything was quiet.

All the people in the hotel were sleeping soundly.

The man was holding a sharp dagger very tightly in one hand. He had no other weapons. The last lamp hanging from the corridor wall spluttered and died, plunging everything into darkness.

The man was thinking hard about the situation. He knew he could just as easily go back the way he had come. There was no need to take any extra precautions. The victim was already a dead body; just the soul still had to fly away.

"Mister" had told him not to try and do anything

courageous, but just to dispose of the person who was causing so many problems. Although it might seem cowardly, the stranger knew very well that it would be impossible to overcome Martin while he was still awake. So nobody wanted to take the risk of disposing with Martin except Mister, and nobody wanted to kill him like a coward either. It was probable that he would sleep all through the next day and night.

The stranger smiled to himself. After a while he found himself standing before the door of room 14. The corridor was plunged in darkness; only a feeble ray of moonlight was illuminating it. The stranger looked swiftly and carefully up and down the corridor. Everything seemed alright. Since it was likely that he would have to run away quickly, he had come barefoot. Still he couldn't dissimulate the occasional creaking of the wooden floorboards. He hoped that the noise would not wake anyone up. The assassin touched the doorknob cautiously. He knew that in somnolent state, Martin would have forgotten to lock the door. He turned the knob slowly and the door opened, proving the stranger absolutely right!

About half an hour later, the moon had disappeared below the horizon and in the darkness of the night no sound could be heard – not a single cricket or the barking of a dog.

"So, Mr. Simpson, I'll give you one more chance to answer my questions," Borhan said to the man sitting on the chair in front of him. The man was dressed only in his underwear and was sweating like a breathless person.

"I-I'm really telling you the truth Sir, believe me!" the man called Simpson stammered.

"You want me to believe me that you were going to the toilet in the middle of the night with a dangerous dagger in your hand?" Borhan asked, waving his six-gun under his nose.

"Ac-actually, not exactly that, Sir. I was going to the toilet alright but I had been thinking of stealing…"

"Why did you choose this room?" Borhan asked in an ice-cold voice.

"How can I convince you Sir? I-I am…" Simpson stopped as he saw Borhan getting up from his chair.

Borhan slapped Simpson hard across the cheek. He pointed at Martin's sleeping body.

"He's my friend," he said. "If I wake him up now and tell him everything that happened, I don't think you'll need to worry about me anymore. So what do you say?"

There were no lights inside the room, but Borhan could make out the man's eyes in the dim moonlight and see that they expressed pure panic. Simpson wiped the sweat from his forehead. It seemed as if he could not decide what to do next. He looked like a restless chimpanzee trapped in a cage.

"So what I'm telling you," Borhan said again, "is that if you can answer my questions properly, then I'll give you the opportunity to escape before this man wakes up. If you want, I won't even mention tonight's incidents."

Simpson thought for a minute. Then he said slowly, "Alright, Sir, tell me what you want to know."

"Yeah, now you're talking sense. But remember – if you try and tell a single lie then I'll cut you into pieces. It's up to you."

Simpson couldn't utter a word and he began to tremble. The man standing in front of him would definitely keep his word – that much was obvious.

"So tell me – who sent you?"

"Mister sent me."

"Mister, who the hell is that?"

"We all call him that."

"Carl, Rust's foreman - does he have anything to do with him?"

"I think they have quite a close relationship, but in front of us other guys, they talk to each other like they were strangers."

"Does he come from Greentown like Carl?"

"Yes, I think so, but I can't say for sure. He always wears a mask in front of us. I've never seen his face."

"I've never seen your face in this town either!"

"Mister hired about five people like me from elsewhere."

"And how many people does he have in all?"

"There must be at least ten people."

"Did he do all the rustling and bank robberies with so few people?"

Simpson did not reply.

Borhan wanted to be sure he was telling the truth.

"But Simpson, where does Mister put all the cattle?"

"They're smuggled to the North in the same round-up and the rancher is told that there is some mistake in the headcount."

"So I guess Carl helps him, doesn't he? That's how thousands of animals could simply disappear under our very noses!"

Borhan was astonished by the procedure. "But Simpson, it's not possible for him to do all that alone – how does he manage for the other ranches?"

"I don't know, I can't really explain."

"Well, explain as well as you can, Simpson."

"As far as I can guess, someone from the *Triple J* ranch must be involved with Carl. But did you know that Carl was captured by the sheriff tonight?"

"Is that so? Very good, that makes things easier for me.

Well, let me ask you one last question - where can I find Mister's gang?"

"If we don't have any assignment, we take cover during the day. But at night, we go to Matthew Rust's ranch. Carl hides us in the bunkhouses and we leave at daybreak."

"Where do you take cover?"

"You know the Pine Tree lake? In the forest there."

"Hm..." Borhan fell silent. He looked at the sleeping figure of Martin and then again at Simpson. He could clearly hear Simpson gulping. The poor man had talked continuously up to then.

"If you don't go back, what will Mister think of you?"

Simpson was scared now.

He shifted uncomfortably in his chair.

"You-you told me that you would let me go Sir..."

"Why are you so scared? I only want to know whether Mister will go for another plan if you don't kill Martin."

"I-I can't say, Sir. B-but Sir, I can't go back. Mister will kill me!"

"OK." Borhan sat on the bed again. "Take your clothes."

"Wi-will you let me go, Sir?" Simpson seemed to hesitate.

"Don't you believe me? Then do this – write a letter to Mister so that he thinks that you were too cowardly to kill Martin and that you're leaving town because you're scared of Mister. Is that OK?"

For the first time, Borhan saw hope in Simpson's eyes, as if he had escaped from death. His pale face came back to life again as he recovered from his fright.

CHAPTER 9

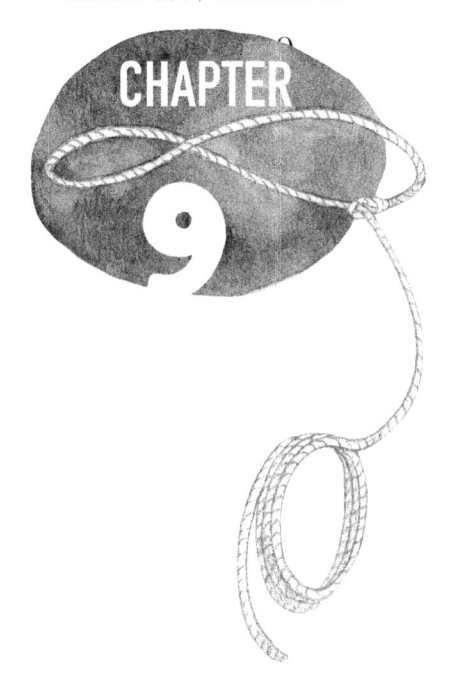

One of the gang member told the others, "Mister has informed us that Carl might speak out at any time."

"But Mister will say goodbye as soon as he's paid us, so we don't need to worry too much about that now."

"Yes, but that's not the main issue. Don't forget that Simpson is missing. We don't even know if he accomplished the work he was sent out for. I think Simpson has been captured and that's why Mister doesn't want to take any more risks. Once we've left, he'll escape as well. Moreover, if Carl blabs out everything he knows about Mister, then we'll be finished too. So we must get away as soon as possible and be careful not to leave any tracks."

"OK, but Mister was supposed to meet us today. The sun will be up in only a couple of hours and people will be about, which will be dangerous for us."

"Don't worry, I think we're safe here. If Carl tells the sheriff about us, then the poor guy will most probably look for us on the other side of the lake and he won't find us there."

"Then...." The man stopped talking.

Someone was knocking at the door. All eyes were immediately riveted on the door.

One of the rustlers went cautiously to the door, his pistol at the ready. "Who is it? David?" Then the rustler pronounced the code.

"No, it's the hostler."

The rustler pulled the door slightly ajar and observed the person behind it. He was certain that it was their man and he reassured the rest of the gang.

Everybody put their guns back into their holsters and relaxed.

As they sat there nonchalantly, the masked person quickly entered the room.

Just thirty seconds later they realised with shock that they had made a terrible mistake!

They remained glued to their seats as it was too late to

react.

A group of gunmen burst into the room, pointing their firearms at the group.

There was no doubt about the stranger's identity - when the man removed his mask, everybody recognised the sheriff.

"Don't be surprised, my friends. I'm the one who brought you here disguised as your Mister. And you have all proved what you deserve by easily falling into my trap. Now, everybody surrender your pistols to my men and come with us like good boys. And don't forget that in the meantime, Mister is preparing more people to kill you guys because we deliberately informed him that we had captured you. He can kill you anytime he wants, for fear that you may inform us about his whereabouts."

There were muffled protests among the rustlers.

"Silence!" the sheriff roared and everybody immediately froze.

"Go and release Mr. Rust's son Vic and send him back to their ranch," the sheriff ordered an armed man beside him. "I'm going to take all this vermin to jail. We'll see who can save Mister from me now!"

The mistress of the *Triple J* ranch, Mrs. Jerri, was pacing impatiently up and down her room. Her face showed a great deal of worry and uncertainty.

Jan was sitting on a chair, rubbing his hands together nervously, and Jenny was standing close by him.

It was well past midnight. It was so quiet you could hear a pin drop. It would soon be another day.

In the room next door, Vic's father, Mr. Rust, was talking with Mr. Jerri. Robertson was there too, leaning against the wall. His son, Johnson, was outside with the ranch crews, who were impatiently waiting with firearms for what was bound to come. At any moment they might be attacked.

"I've made a terrible mistake. All this time I've been sleeping with the enemy, it's ridiculous!" Mr. Rust said in dismay.

"Calm yourself Mathew. Carl will be punished the way he deserves. Let them catch Mister first." Jerri said quietly.

"I've heard that Borhan came to town." Robertson continued. "Now only God knows what will happen!"

"I don't know why, but I have a feeling that Borhan is not involved in any of this," Mathew Rust said. "If he was, then somehow or another I would surely have seen his gang on my ranch. I know every single member of my crew personally, and when I recruited them Carl hadn't yet arrived. You may not know, Jerri, but I brought Carl with me from another place."

"Still, you shouldn't stay alone on your ranch. It's good

that you came to me. If your crews are alright, then your ranch will be alright too."

"I'm rather worried about Vic. I spoke to the sheriff. He was supposed to release Vic, but…."

"Don't worry, I sent one of my men with a letter. He's bound to return with Vic."

"But whatever you say, the sheriff will get every bit of information out of Carl. What a strange name for their boss, *Mister!* Hah!!"

"I think that Carl was going to give plans to Mister to murder you. In that case, I don't think they would spare me either. But even if the sheriff can capture the gang, can he capture Mister too?"

Robertson shook his head. "That brat Mister is surely planning something in secret! He may come and create chaos at any moment."

"You're quite right, Robert. We shouldn't be sitting idle like this. We should help the sheriff…."

"Someone's coming!" Johnson called from outside.

"Maybe it's your son…." Jerri smiled wryly at Mathew Rust, then he ordered sharply, "let him come, it may be Vic!"

Robertson left the room. After a minute or two Vic staggered in with him. They were all shocked to see the state he was in and they ran to hold him up. There was blood all over his body and it was obvious from his face that he had been brutally tortured. His clothes were in shreds.

"The deputy sheriff was going to take him back to the ranch, but on the way they met with our ranch men. There was a big misunderstanding and some shooting. The deputy sheriff and Vic were shot but our crew managed to get them back here safely."

"What? Where did you leave the deputy?" Jerri asked impatiently.

"In the bunkhouse with our crews."

Mrs. Jerri now came into the room and Mathew and Jerri left Vic in her capable hands before going out to the bunkhouse.

#

The deputy sheriff had been badly shot. He was seriously wounded and was fighting with death.
Johnson sat beside him, looking perturbed. When he saw Jerri, he said, "Uncle, this man is trying to say something, but I can't understand him."

Jerri bent down and put his ear close to the man's lips to try and make out what he was saying. The man was whispering with difficulty and his voice was unclear, but the little that Jerri managed to catch made the expression on his face change radically. It was one of complete stupefaction.

Nobody knew what was going on and everyone was staring at Jerri as he stood up slowly.

"Nobody tells a lie before they die," he said. "Quickly send for a doctor and a priest and, Robert, tell the armed forces to be ready immediately. We have to go to town." Then Jerri left the room. Everybody watched him leave with astonishment!

#

It had been a while since the Simpson guy had been sent away. In the meantime, Reeve and Dave had been brought from the hotel, holding naked six-guns.

Borhan was sitting in Martin's room. The latter had eventually woken up, though not without difficulty. Now he was pacing up and down the room.

"You've done a very strange thing!" Borhan remarked, breaking the silence.

Martin stopped walking and stood in front of him.

Then he gave him a sharp glance. "Well you could have warned me, couldn't you?"

"Yes I could, but I didn't know about these girly issues..."

"Look Borhan, stop your silly talk!" Martin stood up straight. He lit a cigar with Dave's help.

Borhan gave him time. "OK, now listen," he said to Martin, "We have some important information. You can be sure that there will be no lack of evidence. You are saved and that is the main thing. Now, please prepare yourself mentally."

Martin nodded at him.

He pointed at his pistol and asked to have it back.

Borhan handed it to him, he put it in his holster and in exchange gave Borhan his cigar.

"I'm ready. Do we start now?"

"Yes," Borhan replied, drawing on the cigar. "But remember, we have to catch Mister alive."

"There will be no harm done to him. What about you?"

"We have our men at the *Triple J* ranch. Though ironically, Simpson..."

"Simpson...?"

"That rustler, just a while ago who was... well, if he was telling us the truth, then there may be a bit of a fight. But it shouldn't spread to the house."

"What about Carl?"

"I guess he's dead by now. But Vic has been released," Reeve announced, nonchalantly. "I saw him a little while ago...."

"Wait a minute!" Martin exclaimed. "Vic has been released and in the meantime Carl is dead... What are you telling me?"

"It's quite simple," Borhan replied. "Carl was poisoned with his dinner, because Mister had to do something that the townsfolk could believe in order to shut him up. At the same time, he has probably planned something for his own gang so that he can hide somewhere. It's certain that he suspects us because he knows very well that we will have recognised him by now. He thinks we don't have any proof against him, and so we want to catch his companions. So he..."

"So if he thinks that, he would deliberately kill his companions." Martin interrupted Borhan, "If we can't capture his men, then we won't be able to capture him either, am I right?"

"Absolutely. And he must be putting these ideas into action somewhere right now!"

"Then let's go immediately, we mustn't waste any more time." Martin headed towards the door. Just then they heard the townspeople cheering. The noise penetrated the silence of the night. There were some sounds of shooting too.

"So the game has begun," Dave murmured.

CHAPTER 10

There was a large crowd in front of the sheriff's office. Everyone was shouting excitedly. Only a few minutes before they had been sleeping soundly, but now they were calling out impatiently to learn more.

The moonlight penetrated the darkness of the night, clearly illuminating everything all around.

"Dear friends!" the sheriff addressed the townsfolk, "we are finally going to succeed after all our attempts. It has taken some time, but we have now successfully captured the rustlers who were responsible for creating all the unrest in town. We still need to catch the leader of the gang, but I'm sure if you help us, that shouldn't take too long."

"We're ready and willing to help!" many of the onlookers called out.

"Thank you. You all know that these people have been making trouble in town in many ways, robbing the bank and cattle rustling… What do you think would be proper punishment for them?"

"Hang them all!" somebody proposed vociferously.

"Let them bathe in their own blood!" others shouted.

The sheriff raised his hand to stop them, "Your wish will be granted. But before that, help me find the person who is behind all this. Help me get the information out of them!"

"Your wish will be granted as well!" the people promised.

"Then wait until dawn. In the meantime, I'll find a way to capture the gang leader by interrogating his men."

The sheriff went back into his office, satisfied with the townspeople's reaction.

The crowd gradually broke up and people started to return home. The sheriff's deputies remained near the jailhouse, guarding it with their guns.

Martin and Borhan watched everything from afar and were reassured by the way the sheriff was managing the situation. Even so, they knew that he was taking a risk by putting Mister's people behind bars.

They went to the office.

The sheriff looked up when he heard the door opening. He smiled while he saw Borhan entering the office, but was surprised to see Martin with him.

"Hey Borhan, come along! I was waiting for you, I knew you'd come."

They looked at the scared faces of the prisoners. There were about ten of them. But their eyes soon became riveted on a dead body on the floor, covered with a white sheet.

It must be Carl's corpse.

"Sit down," the sheriff invited. "There's nothing new to tell. You can see with your own eyes." The sheriff gestured towards the prisoners.

"Yes, it's all obvious. But how did it happen… and this dead body…?" Borhan surveyed and asked.

"That's Carl. He was the one who informed me about their hiding place and who gave me Mister's description. I tricked them into coming to town and then captured them. On the way back, I saw that Carl had been poisoned…" The sheriff paused. "I found a dead body in the meadows - it was my deputy. I had ordered him to release Vic from jail, so I'm not sure what happened."

"I understand. But what are you doing about the real

criminal?" Borhan wanted to know.

"First have a look to see if there is anyone on your list as well. Here, do it quickly!" Sheriff handed him the list.

Everyone turned towards the door as one of the guards came in.

"Sir, a group of riders are heading this way," he announced. "What should we do?"

"Let them come and don't create any trouble," the sheriff replied. "But keep a close eye on them, so that they can't come in here with weapons."

The deputy left to carry out the orders. The sheriff smiled at Borhan and Martin. "We'd better be careful. Who knows, maybe the stranger really is this 'Mister'."

They all remained silent.

All of sudden, some shots rang out.

#

Reeve and Dave emerged stealthily from the dark bushes around the jailhouse. Something was flashing in the moonlight.

Razor blades!

They parted ways to approach their victims from two different angles, like reapers.

Dave was able to fell a man at his very first attempt and a second man was swiftly brought to the ground by Reeve. There had been two other men standing by the jailhouse window; they had both been silenced as well. Reeve's and Dave's hands were red with blood.

They wiped their hands with their handkerchiefs.

The razor blade had done its gory work.

Their pistols were at the ready as they waited for the signal.

There were four more soldiers in front of the jailhouse who had to be dealt with. As Reeve and Dave waited for the signal, a volley of shots penetrated the silence of the night! Immediately afterwards, Reeve fell to the ground with a large hole in his head. Dave was startled, but quickly threw himself to the ground to protect himself.

A bullet whistled over his head and he responded right away with a bullet of his own. The bullets were coming from the front side of the jail.

Suddenly the shooting stopped and was replaced by the sound of horse's hooves. Dave prepared himself. He took the pistol that had fallen from Reeve's hand and started crawling to a safer place where he could take cover.

But in the end he could not save himself....

He had run out of ammunition.

"Put your hands up!" the sheriff ordered in a calm but firm voice.

He was pointing his gun at Martin and Borhan.

They remained speechless.

Shortly before, the gang of rustlers had been in prison, but now they were all outside with guns in their hands.

The sheriff ordered two of them to search Martin and Borhan, but they found nothing in particular.

The sheriff seemed surprised.

"What's wrong my friends, how come you're going round without any weapons?"

Borhan smiled. "Yeah, I suppose it was rather foolish of us!"

The sheriff raised his eyebrows.

"Don't you think you were a little too foolhardy? If you really knew who I was, then why did you come deliberately into the lion's den?"

"Maybe we wouldn't have come if we had known that you would show your real face so quickly," Martin replied.

There was no more shooting.

The sheriff looked at his men.

"My friends," he said, "we need to help our people outside. Go and fetch them and tell them that the gunfight has been postponed. I have something to do first."

Some of the rustlers left to obey his orders.

The sheriff looked at Martin and Borhan again.

"What do you have in mind, sheriff?" Borhan asked him.

"Right now I want to kill you two!" the sheriff said, with

his hand on the trigger.

"Hey wait a minute! Why are you acting so quickly? There are still things we want to know!"

"I'm not going to waste my time answering your silly questions!"

"Well that's strange! If you already knew that we suspected you, then you could have finished us a long time ago without wasting your valuable time, sheriff!"

"That's right, but I needed you."

"What do you mean?"

"I've used you for my own ends. You couldn't possibly guess that. I allowed Borhan to stay in town, and you, Martin, I introduced you to the townspeople in such a way that they all suspect you to be a bounty hunter who came here in search of a terrible criminal. Of course, the reason is almost true for you, although without your bounty hunter identity. I know very well that you are really U.S. Marshal Harry Laslore!"

"Very strange!" Martin was really surprised. "But what could you accomplish with all this?"

Borhan intervened. "He used his own people to make trouble and then blamed and captured my people instead. Rustling, bank robbery – he did all that just to make people think that someone was trying to destroy Greentown. At the same time, he pretended to be an honest and just person by staging their arrest!"

"You're absolutely right!" There was an evil smile on the sheriff's face. "But to be honest, Martin - sorry, Harry - wasn't expected here at all. His arrival thwarted my plans. But I didn't know that he had been brought here by you, Borhan. I only realised that when you told me that you were staying at Saliman's hotel. So I sent a man to put some poison pills in his supper which could kill him. I guessed that if you really had any connection with Harry then you would try and save him, and things went just as I expected. Because of that, I realised that you must suspect that I would kill my own people to save myself."

"But why did you kill Carl?"

"I had to get rid of him one way or another because sometimes I spoke to him without my mask. He was the only one who could identify me. Also, it was due to his carelessness that you came here. Tell me, Borhan," the sheriff continued, "why did you bring Martin to Greentown? Was it because of the unrest?"

"No. I found out that you had been in another town in the West before coming here, but your movements or location couldn't be traced. That's why I brought Harry here, so that he could observe each and every individual in the town and see if anyone had a criminal background. As a matter of fact, Harry identified you on the very first day; he told me that you used to kill people for money. From then on, I knew that people had made a terrible mistake by putting you in a position of authority, to protect the town, when you were actually the one responsible for destroying everything."

"Hahaha!" The sheriff laughed loudly and rather manically. "The protector is the one who destroys! Hahaha!!"

"You've laughed enough, Dalton!" expostulated Borhan with disgust. "I was an outlaw once too. I've killed dozens of people when necessary. But I've never seen a brat like you!"

"You never saw one before, but you've seen one now!" Martin alias Harry Laslore exclaimed. "Forget it, Borhan, we got our answers. Dalton, you can shoot us now without another thought!"

Sheriff Dalton never imagined that Harry would say such a thing. The smile was wiped off his face. He clenched his pistol and looked at them suspiciously.

"Wait a minute! I think I may have understood something... It's not possible that wild wolves like you can surrender so easily to their fate." Dalton stood up slowly. "... which can only mean that the people my men were fighting were actually your men? But... but what about the men that I ordered to attack you here?"

"What do you mean?" Harry and Borhan said together.

"I knew that you two would come here. So I told them to

come and attack you. I would...."

"You would wound us and disguise us as 'Mister' so that you could implement your plan," Martin interrupted him. "Your strategies are fantastic, Dalton, I'm very impressed!" Martin said, although his tone sounded more insulting than impressed. Ignoring Dalton's gun, he stood up and looked the "Sheriff" straight in the eye. "But now the game's over!"

Dalton didn't have the time to press the trigger.

Martin alias Harry pressed a handful of strychnine powder on his face. At the same time, he scattered more strychnine powder that he had dissimulated in his boots over the startled rustlers.

He had kept Dalton busy talking, while he quietly removed his boots.

In just a couple of minutes everyone was motionless.

They had all crashed to the ground, struggled feebly, and then lost consciousness.

Harry and Borhan had to hold their breath so as not to inhale the powder, but they soon breathed a sigh of relief and looked at each other with satisfaction.

#

There was a huge crowd in front of the jailhouse.

Altogether there were twelve dead bodies on the premises.

In the middle of all the chaos, Borhan was weeping

silently over the bodies of Dave and Reeve.

The undertaker had been called to remove the corpses while the town authorities took the unconscious criminals to be imprisoned. Word soon got around that Martin Laslore was in fact U.S. Marshal Harry Laslore.

Harry wasn't interested. He had started out towards the *Triple J* ranch.

CHAPTER 11

"You shouldn't take the risk, Jerri. There might be ambushers lying in wait." Mathew Rust was sitting beside the unconscious and wounded Vic.

"I'll leave Johnson to protect you," Mr. Jerri said as he checked his gun belt. "You can go with your son."

Then he murmured to himself, "That brat is trying to take over everything himself. He wants to be the king alone! I'm going to put an end to that today!"

"I can't believe that the person we gave the responsibility to protect our town is actually the one who..." Jenny made a regretful sound. She was sitting beside her mother. "And we all trusted him like fools!"

The door opened and Robertson appeared, looking

agitated.

"Jerri! A gang is hiding around the ranch. They've killed two of our men!"

Robertson was shocked. As soon as he stopped talking, there was a sound of shooting outside.

"You all stay here. Don't go outside, I'm going to see what's going on," said Jerri, going into the next room with Robertson.

Two of the trustworthy crews were standing outside with their firearms. The window panes had been shattered by the assailants and the crews were responding.

"Where's Johnson?" Jerri asked.

"In the bunk house. They have no more bullets left. And we couldn't go to the cartridge room either. There were some traitors among our men."

"What?" Jerri said in despair.

"Yes, it looks like there were five of them."

There were no lights on in the room, but in the moonlight Jerri suddenly caught sight of a shadow, which quickly hid on the other side of the lake. Another shadow came out of the bunk house, but was quickly felled. That meant that Johnson and the others were trapped there.

"Robert, we can't stay here like this any longer," Jerri said. "We won't survive. There are no more bullets left in the six-guns; we must decide what to do very quickly."

The two crews were shooting at intervals. Robert told them to stop. He was thinking fast.

Jerri stood by the window to give him time to think up a plan.

He looked outside to try and assess the situation.

The shooting had stopped and there was no other noise from outside. Suddenly there was a moving shadow and a loud scream.

"Come out with your hands up, or else...."

Another shot was fired and Jerri saw that shadow had fallen to the ground. People were running towards the ranch house. Before Jerri could fire at them, they fell to the ground under another shower of bullets. At the same time, the bunkhouse door was flung open and Johnson and the other men appeared.

Jerri and Robertson could see someone else approaching from the very spot where the assailants were hiding. The moonlight lit his face. It was Martin Laslore!

#

Two days later in Greentown, there was great rejoicing. Once a dangerous outlaw, Borhan, was now elected as sheriff with an overwhelming majority of votes. To celebrate, there was a reception in the Town Hall. Harry Laslore was sitting beside Borhan on the stage.

A few rows ahead, Jenny was sitting on the guest seat and busy talking with other girls. Johnson could be seen with some other guys on the other side.

Borhan and Harry both saw that Jenny and Johnson were speaking to each other with their eyes.

"They're looking great, aren't they?" Martin alias Harry commented with a smile. Borhan smiled back, but did not reply.

"It's a shame I can't be present at their wedding," Harry continued, raising his glass of champagne as a toast to the happy couple. Just then Harry felt Jenny's eyes on him. He looked back at her, a little ruefully.

Harry had to return to California to start a new life. He would probably have to visit other places like Greentown. And maybe someone like Jenny would be waiting for him there.

Maybe.

The End

ABOUT THE AUTHOR

I use *Uncle Nafee* as a pseudonym. I born in Bangladesh, the country that fought for their mother language in 1952 and independence in 1971. My first book was published in 2005. I then published several more original hardcover mystery, thriller, horror & ghost fiction books in Bengali and edited a few hardcover anthologies in the same category. I have contributed my versatile abilities to an illustrated print horror fiction magazine as an editor and publisher. One of my story was adapted into a television drama. I now live in the United Kingdom and trying to pursue my career in writing.

A few more books in English:

A Secret Behind The Bungalow (audiobook & hardback)
Strange Serious Short Stories SsSs... (paperback)
Uncanny Episodes (paperback)

Printed in Great Britain
by Amazon